GODFATHER CAT AND MOUSIE

DORIS ORGEL

Retold after the Brothers Grimm

illustrations by

ANN SCHWENINGER

Macmillan Publishing Company · New York

Macmillan Publishing Company
866 Third Avenue, New York, N.Y. 10022
Collier Macmillan Canada, Inc.
Printed and bound by South China Printing Company, Hong Kong
First American Edition

10 9 8 7 6 5 4 3 2 1

The text of this book is set in 14 pt. ITC Cushing Book.
The illustrations are rendered in watercolor.

Library of Congress Cataloging in Publication Data
Orgel, Doris.
Godfather Cat and Mousie.
Summary: A cat and mouse live together in harmony until
it is revealed that a hungry cat can't be trusted.
[1. Fairy tales.   2. Folklore—Germany]
I. Schweninger, Ann, ill.   II. Title.
PZ8.067Go   1986   398.2′452′0943 [E]   85-10567
ISBN 0-02-768690-6

Remembering Ernest Adelberg
—D.O.

For Debby L. Carter
—A.S.

Once a smooth and handsome cat met a little mouse. "Come live with me," he begged her. "I'll care for you. I'll keep you company. Please, please, pretty Mousie."

So she moved in. They set up house together.

When autumn came, the cat said, "Mousie, let's go
buy something we can eat in winter when food is hard
to find."

Out they went and bought a pot of cream.

"Where shall we keep it?" asked the mouse.

The cat had an idea: "Why not in the church? No one would dare to steal from there. We'll hide it under the altar and not go near it till we need it."

They hid the cream pot there.

One morning when the cat woke up, his mouth felt very dry. "Mousie," he said, "my cousin had a little son, white with brown flecks, and she wants me to be his godfather. Do you mind if I go out today while you stay and see to the house?"

"Of course not," said the mouse. "Enjoy yourself. Just think of me a little bit if there are good things to eat and drink."

The cat said, "Yes, I will."

Now, the truth is, the cat had no cousins. Off he went to the church, straight to the cream pot, and started to lick. And he licked the thick, sweet top off.

Afterward he took a stroll along the rooftops of the
town, enjoying all the sights. Then he stretched out in

the sun and wiped his moustache contentedly, thinking
of the good sweet cream now inside his belly.

It was evening when he returned.

The mouse was glad to see him. "Did you have a jolly day?"

"Yes, thank you, very jolly."

"What did they name your godchild?"

"Topoff," said the cat.

"Topoff? Isn't that outlandish?"

"No," said the cat, "not nearly so outlandish as Crumbstealer—*your* godchild's name, good Mousie."

Another morning before long, the cat's mouth felt dry again. "Mousie," he said, "another of my cousins has had a child and asked that I be godfather. This child has a white ring around his neck, so I can hardly refuse."

"Of course not," the mouse agreed.

Off went the cat to the church and licked the cream half up. "Nothing's so yummy as a treat savored in secret," he remarked, very pleased with himself.

"What did they name the child?" asked the mouse when the cat returned.

"Halfup," answered he.

"Halfup? You don't say! I never heard that name in my life." Nor did she like the sound of it.

One morning not long after, the cat's mouth felt drier than ever. "Mousie," he said, "all good things come in threes. Still another cat child was born. As happens ever so rarely, this one is entirely black—not a single white hair—except for white paws. You *will* let me go and be godfather, won't you?"

"Hmm," mused the mouse, "Topoff, Halfup—such curious names make me wonder."

"Don't wonder too much," said the cat, and off he went.

The mouse took his advice. She didn't wonder too much. She was too hungry for that. She looked in the larder for something to eat, and then in all the cupboards.

She grew more and more hungry, and finally she started to nibble the wall.

Meanwhile the cat licked the cream in the cream pot all up.

"What did they name your third godchild?" asked the mouse.

"You won't like this name any better than the other two," warned the cat. "Allup."

"Allup?" cried the mouse. "Amazing!" And she thought about it a lot.

Winter came, and there was nothing to eat, inside or out. "Now let's go to our cream pot that we hid away," said the mouse. "Come, Cat. Think how tasty."

"As tasty as if you hung your fine, dainty tongue out the window," replied the cat, not budging from his armchair.

"What a very strange reply," said the mouse. "Come, Cat, let us go."

But the cat would not.

"What can it mean?" the mouse thought aloud. "First top off, next half up, then…"

"Be still," said the cat. "One more word and I'll eat you…"

"All up!" was on the tip of the mouse's tongue. No sooner did she utter it than—*some* people say—the cat in one leap snatched her up and gulped her down, for that's how it goes in the world.

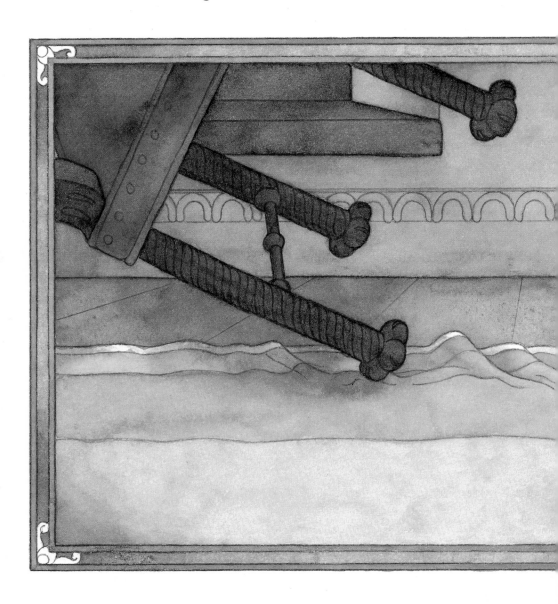

But here's what *I* say happened, and maybe you'll agree.

While the cat was leaping, the mouse, quick as a wink, ran into the hole she'd nibbled in the wall. She'd nibbled right on through, you see, and into the next house. So that is where she ran.

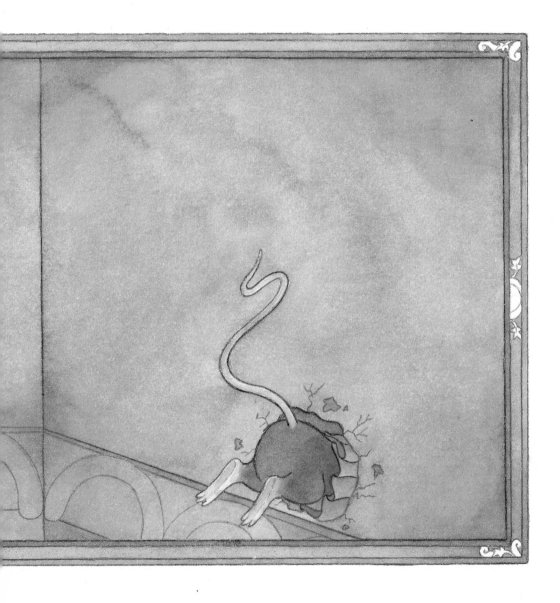

And that is where her cousins lived. For the truth is, the mouse had cousins galore and many, many godchildren, too many to count. Crumbstealer, Fatsnatcher, Rindfinder, and plump little Cheesenibbler are the names of only a few.

"Welcome, welcome," they all squeaked when she
came streaking in.

They held a party in her honor.
They feasted on finest breadcrumbs, crunchiest
bacon (not just the rinds), rich good bits of butter,

and cheese of every kind—cheddar, Gouda,
Liederkranz, Edam, and Swiss. All they left
were the holes.

As for the cat, if he did not die of shame, he's still keeping watch by the hole in the wall, waiting for his Mousie to this day.

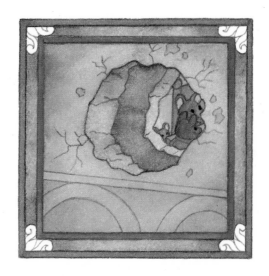